Also by HERTHA PAULI

The First Christmas Tree
The First Easter Rabbit

Author's note:

This story sounds as if it were too marvelous to be true,
but it is all fact. Every incident of this Christmas of 1492
was reported by Christopher Columbus in his Journal.
There he records exactly how the Santa Maria was
wrecked, and how generous the Indians were. The gold
and the tinkling bells, the mask and the words of King
Guacanagari and Columbus — all are authentic.

Ives Washburn, Inc., New York

America's First Christmas

by HERTHA PAULI
pictures by FRITZ KREDEL

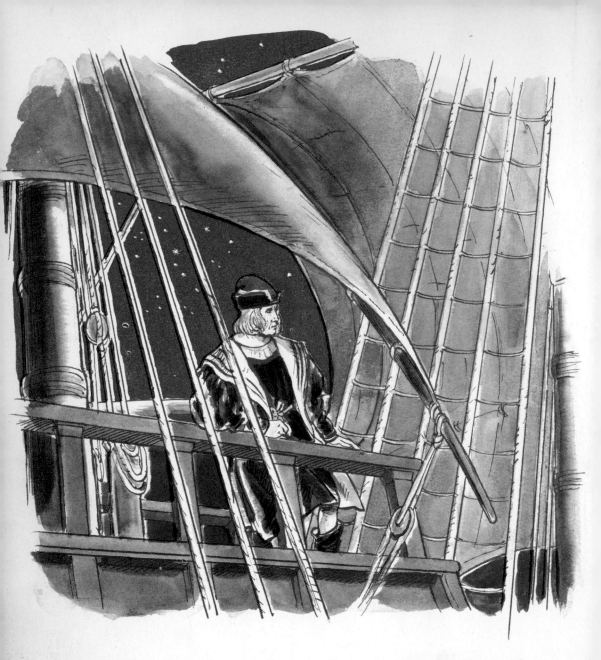

It was Christmas Eve, in the year 1492. A proud
little ship was sailing toward a new shore.

Her name was *Santa Maria*. The flag of the Queen
of Spain flew from her mast, and on her quarterdeck stood the Admiral, Christopher Columbus.
He had blue eyes, and hair bleached almost white
by the sun and the sea.

By the dim light of the stars he watched his second ship, the *Niña*, leading the way from the ocean into a beautiful, quiet bay. His third ship, the *Pinta*, had been out of sight for some time. But this did not worry Columbus, for he knew that his little fleet had safely crossed the Sea of Darkness all the way from Spain. In the bay the wind died down, and the only sound was the roll of the surf on distant coral reefs.

Then a song rang out in the silent night.

> The watch is called,
> The glass floweth
> We shall have a good voyage
> If God willeth!

Two ship-boys, little Pedro and big Juan, were singing the song as they changed the night watch.

Columbus smiled. Every night since midsummer he had heard this song when the watch changed at eleven o'clock — and now it was Christmas Eve. A long journey, he thought, and, if God wills, a successful one. He bowed his head and prayed: "We thank you, Our Lord, for another day's safe sailing, and for sending Your Son to our world this night."

When Columbus looked up again, he saw Juan reach for the sand clock, which hung from a beam near the tiller. The sand clock was a tall glass, pinched in the middle and half filled with sand.

Each time the sand had run from the top to the bottom of the glass a ship-boy had to turn it upside down again.

Another hour had passed. Pedro marked it on a chart. This was how they told time on the *Santa Maria*.

"It will be Christmas in just an hour," said Juan.

Pedro looked up to see if he could find the Christmas Star in this strange world.

"What are you looking for, my boy?" asked a deep voice. Christopher Columbus stood before his ship-boys.

"I am looking for the Christmas Star," Pedro answered. "Which one is it?"

"They all are Christmas Stars tonight," Columbus said, as he looked up at the sky. "Did we not follow the stars through the Sea of Darkness? Their light guided us here."

For a moment all three gazed at the countless stars. Pedro remembered the storms in the endless ocean they had crossed from Spain. The sailors called it the Sea of Darkness. For weeks they had feared they were lost in these unknown waters.

"Yes," Pedro said in a low voice, "the stars guided us here."

"But the people here don't know about Christmas," Juan said sadly.

"Then we must bring Christmas to them," Columbus told Pedro and Juan. He looked once more at the sea around them. "The sea here is as calm as the water in a cup," he said. "We will have a quiet holy night. Now I can rest. I am very tired." He wished the boys good night and "Feliz Navidad" —which is Spanish for "Merry Christmas."

And Columbus went below to his cabin.

Pedro followed their beloved Admiral with his eyes. He was like a father to the boys and a friend to everyone. He even tried to make friends with the natives, whom he and his men called Indians. They had learned to understand each other and communicated by signs and a few words.

"How can we bring Christmas to the Indians?" little Pedro asked big Juan.

"The Admiral must know," Juan replied. "He knows everything," he added with admiration. "Didn't he find a way through the Sea of Darkness, where no sailor dared go before?"

"Yes," Pedro agreed. "He showed us the new way to India, sailing westward on and on around the world."

Never would Pedro forget the day when they first reached land—it was the twelfth of October. The Admiral had led them ashore on a strange island, where he had thanked God for making his dream come true. He was sure, he told them, that they had reached India.

"We found the way," said big Juan, "but we didn't find the gold the Admiral is looking for."

Pedro nodded. He knew that the Admiral had promised the Queen of Spain to bring her the gold of India. "Will we ever find gold?" he wondered.

"I'm sure we will," Juan answered. "We just have to find some Indians who know where it is."

Pedro sighed. Again and again they had asked the Indians where to find gold. Again and again the Indians had sent them on to other islands. From island to island they had sailed, on and on, since October. And now it was Christmas Eve....

For the first time Pedro felt homesick. "I wish I were home tonight," he murmured.

"At least we are safe tonight," Juan replied. "I'm tired now." He looked around the deck. "Here is a good spot to sleep." And he stretched out on a folded sail.

Now Pedro had no one to talk to. Instead of watching the sand clock here on Christmas Eve, he could have been at home with his family placing the little figures in the Christmas Crib. There would be Mary and Joseph, kneeling before the manger, and the shepherds with their sheep, watching the stable. And the Three Wise Men who had followed the Christmas Star, bringing gifts for the Christ Child — all would be there, as they had been on every Christmas Pedro could remember.

Then the bells would ring out merrily for church, and people from near and far would join to worship....

With tears in his eyes Pedro gazed at the glittering stars. If I cannot help light the candles at home, he thought, perhaps I can help to bring Christmas to the Indians.

Silently the sand dropped through the glass. Gentle waves rocked the *Santa Maria* like a cradle. It was very quiet.

Pedro saw the Captain yawning. "Helmsman," he heard him call to the man who was steering the ship, "just follow the *Niña!* Wake me only if the weather changes." And the Captain, too, went to his cabin.

As soon as he had disappeared, the sailors on watch began to look for comfortable spots on deck. One after the other lay down and dropped off to sleep.

Next the helmsman gave a big yawn. Then he turned to Pedro. "Come here, boy," he ordered.

"Take the helm. I can't stand up any longer. It is easy to steer through this calm bay. Just follow the *Niña*. I'll watch from nearby." He turned the tiller over to Pedro and lay down in the steerage.

Trembling with excitement Pedro gripped the heavy helm. He knew that no boy was allowed to steer the ship. What could he do? He must obey the helmsman. So Pedro tried to follow the *Niña*. But from the dark, low steerage he could not see her white sails. He was too small.

He called the helmsman — and was answered by a snore. On the whole ship no one was awake but Pedro!

All he could do was to keep the tiller straight and watch the sand clock. Soon he saw the last grains drop from the top to the bottom of the glass. Christmas has come, he thought, and he heard the church bells ringing all the way from home....

Suddenly the ringing swelled in his ears to a roaring sound. It was not the Christmas bells from home but the surf right beneath the *Santa Maria*. The heavy tiller swung to one side and with all his strength Pedro could not turn it back. He cried out.

The sleeping sailors jumped up and stumbled around in confusion. "What has happened?" shouted the helmsman.

"We are sliding on a coral reef!" the Admiral thundered as he reached the quarterdeck. "We are aground!"

Pedro's heart stood still. "Forgive me," he faltered. "Please, forgive me—" But no one listened.

Still half asleep, the Captain appeared.

"You are responsible, Captain," Columbus shouted. "How could you let a boy steer this ship? Now lower the boat and try to drag us off this reef!"

The Captain and his men put the boat into the water. Pedro watched them climb in and take the oars. Then he gasped with surprise. Instead of trying to free the *Santa Maria*, they rowed off toward the *Niña!*

"Our boat is gone," Pedro cried, "our only boat!"

In cold anger the Admiral turned back to the rest of the crew. "Cut down the main mast," he commanded. "We must lighten the ship to get her afloat."

Tears ran down Pedro's cheeks as he saw the proud mast fall. This must help, he thought. But the tide had just turned and the waves drove the *Santa Maria* higher and higher up on the reef.

God help us, Pedro prayed. He saw the sand clock swing from the beam. I forgot to turn it, he remembered. Everything I do is wrong. Now we don't even know what time it is.

Suddenly Juan cried: "Look, Pedro, help is coming!" And he pointed at two boats approaching the ship.

"At least you are back," Columbus called down to the Captain who returned in the first boat.

"And I brought the *Niña's* boat with me," the Captain answered.

But it was too late now to free the *Santa Maria*. The sharp edges of the coral rocks were punching holes in her wooden timbers. Water came pouring in.

Columbus sighed. "We must abandon ship," he decided. "But all the men will be saved," he went on. "Captain, take the crew to the *Niña*."

The two boats could only carry a few at a time, so the Captain ordered the ship-boys to go first. Pedro watched Juan and the others climb over the side and slide down a rope to the boat.

"Come on, Pedro," Juan called from the boat. "Hurry up!"

Pedro shook his head. "I steered our ship on the reef," he called back, "I can't leave her now." From the rail he watched the boats push off and disappear in the dark.

The two boats made many trips back and forth between the *Santa Maria* and the *Niña*. When the first daylight appeared above the water the Admiral came down from the quarterdeck and found Pedro standing by the rail.

"Why are you still here, my boy?" Columbus asked.

"It's my fault that our ship is aground," Pedro replied in a trembling voice. "I want to stay with you."

The Admiral put his arm around Pedro's shoulders. "It is not your fault, Pedro," was his kind answer. "You did the best you could. And now we will save what we can." Then the Admiral turned to the helmsman. "When the boats come back," he commanded, "take one and row ashore to ask the Indians for help. We need more boats to save the cargo." He pointed at Pedro. "Take this boy with you and try your best."

So in the dawn of Christmas Day little Pedro went ashore with the helmsman on a mission. The sun was rising as they landed. At first Pedro saw nothing but green jungle and tall palm trees. Then a group of Indians appeared and came forward with friendly gestures. Their brown skin was painted with bright colors and they wore long feathers on their heads.

The tallest of all was their King, Guacanagari. He welcomed his visitors with a cheerful smile. But when he understood about the shipwreck tears filled his eyes.

"I will do all I can to help you," he promised.

Immediately he ordered his men into their canoes. All of them went out to the *Santa Maria*. And when the canoes came back they were loaded with tools and clothing and food from the ship. The Indians stared in admiration at all these wonderful things.

I hope that nothing will be taken, Pedro worried. Then he saw the King keeping close watch to be sure that all was safe.

Some little bells particularly delighted the Indians. They picked them up and made them tinkle. "Chuque, chuque," they said, trying to imitate the sound of the bells.

"Put those tinkling things down," the King ordered sternly. And his men were quick to obey.

Back and forth from ship to shore the Indians paddled in their canoes all through Christmas Day.

The sinking sun cast a golden glow on the sea as Christopher Columbus arrived in the boat from the *Niña*. He carried in his hands the flag of the Queen of Spain.

Pedro ran toward the boat, and suddenly he saw Juan there, too, waving his cap at him.

Pedro waved back. "Why are you here?" he called.

Juan laughed. "The *Niña* was not big enough for all of us," he called back and jumped out of the boat.

King Guacanagari welcomed the Admiral warmly and showed him the cargo which he had so carefully guarded. Deeply moved, Columbus thanked the King and his men for their wonderful help.

"Chuque, chuque," the Indians answered and pointed at the tinkling bells.

"Fill their hands with our little bells," Columbus said to the boys.

Juan and Pedro hurried to obey.

"Please keep one little bell for me," the Indian King told the Admiral, "and I shall give you a beautiful mask with big eyes and ears of shining yellow."

The mask was presented!

Pedro could hardly believe his eyes, and the Admiral, too, looked at the mask in great surprise. Could these eyes and ears be made of gold?

Christopher Columbus turned to King Guacanagari. "Do you really wish to give me this wonderful mask with four pieces of shining gold for one little bell?" he asked.

The King smiled graciously. "Yes, I do," he answered. "I want to make you forget the loss of your ship."

Pedro saw the Admiral's blue eyes light up as he and the King exchanged these presents.

"If you like the yellow metal," King Guacanagari went on, "you can find as much as you want of it here. And all I have is yours."

"Now we'll get the gold for the Queen," Juan whispered to Pedro.

"And soon we'll be able to go home," Pedro whispered back.

Columbus thanked the King. "You are turning the loss of my ship into good fortune," he exclaimed. "It must have been the hand of God that steered the *Santa Maria* onto the reef!"

Pedro felt jubilant — now he knew that he was really forgiven!

Still another Christmas surprise was to come. The King invited all his visitors to share his meal in a clearing before his palace. Although it was nothing but a hut decked with palm leaves, Columbus and his crew were served the best food they had eaten since they left Spain.

There were sweet potatoes, such as Juan and Pedro had never tasted before, delicious lobster and other tempting seafoods, and Indian bread.

"What a feast," said Juan and took a second helping.

"What a treat," added Pedro. "We wanted to bring Christmas to the Indians—but without knowing it, they have brought it to us!"

Then Columbus rose to speak. "It must be God's will," he declared, "that we found a settlement here. Not all of us can return on the *Pinta* and the *Niña*. Out of the wreck of the *Santa Maria* we shall build a fort to defend this lovely island from all enemies."

King Guacanagari was delighted with the idea.

Columbus decided to leave all the supplies of the *Santa Maria* and most of her crew to defend their first settlement, and to find more and more gold for the Queen of Spain.

"Would you like to stay?" Juan asked Pedro.

Pedro couldn't quite make up his mind. Before he was ready to answer, the King asked Columbus: "Will you stay with us?"

Columbus shook his head. "I shall sail home on the *Niña* with the boys and the rest of my men to report to the Queen," he said.

Pedro clapped his hands with joy.

"We are going to miss you," the King told Columbus.

"We shall be back soon," promised the Admiral. "And the name of our first settlement shall remind us forever of the wonderful welcome we found here on Christmas Day." The fort, he went on to say, shall be called *LA NAVIDAD* — Spanish for Christmas.

Little Pedro and big Juan agreed that they would never forget this Christmas!

Before they all went to sleep in the hammocks of the Indians, late this Christmas Day, Columbus prepared a report for the Queen of Spain. "These people do love their neighbors as themselves," he wrote. "I assure Your Highness, there is no better people and no better land in all the world."

But Christopher Columbus never learned that this land was not India. He had in fact discovered a new world—the world we call America. And the name he gave his little fort, *LA NAVIDAD*, still reminds us of America's first Christmas.